Smiles and hugs given HERE!

I meant to do that!

Happier than a hippo in a hoop skirt

Stay Cool

This
Doc McStuffins
Annual
belongs to

_____

_____

age _____

Need a cuddle?

Annual 2015

Contents

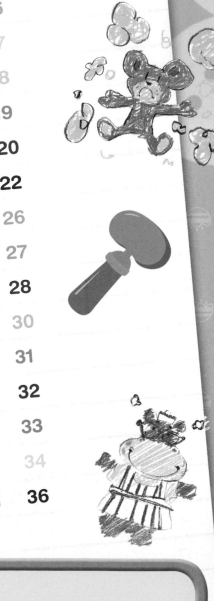

EGMONT

We bring stories to life

First published in 2013 by Egmont UK Limited.
This reissue edition published in Great Britain 2014.
Published by Egmont UK Limited, 1 Nicholas Road, London W11 4AN.

PLEASE NOTE: this edition has the same content as the Doc McStuffins Annual 2014 which was available through an exclusive retailer in 2013.

Activities and story adaptations by Brenda Apsley.
Designed by Jeannette O'Toole.
Created for Egmont UK Ltd by Ruby Shoes Limited.
© 2014 Disney Enterprises, Inc. All rights reserved.

ISBN 978 1 4052 7203 2
57510/2

"Hi! The Doc is in! Let's be friends!"

Say Hi to Doc and Her Friends

Six year old Doc McStuffins is a doctor for stuffed animals and toys. If they have a problem, Doc can fix them, and take the ouchies away! **"Boo-boos be gone!"** she says.

And guess what? Doc can bring toys to life! She uses her magic stethoscope to make them walk and talk, just like you! But this is a BIG secret, so don't tell anyone, will you?

Because it's a secret, when anyone comes near, Doc says, **"Toys, go stuffed!"** and her friends go back to being toys again.

Doc knows all about toys, but what do you know about Doc? Write ✔ true or ✗ false.

1 Doc is a vet. ☐

2 Doc has a magic stethoscope. ☐

3 Doc is 6 years old. ☐

Lambie the lamb is Doc's Best Friend Forever. She loves singing, dancing, and giving cuddles. She hates getting dirty.

Need a cuddle? ❀

Stuffy the dragon is a little bit clumsy, but he pretends he's not! When he bumps into things he says, "I meant to do that!"

Rrrrroar!

Hallie the hippo loves being helpful, and she looks after Doc's clinic. She always has Doc's equipment ready when she needs it.

Here to help!

Chilly the snowman often thinks there's something wrong with him. He feels better when Doc gives him a check-up and tells him he's OK.

Brrrrrrr! Chill on out!

Can you answer yes or no to these questions about Doc's friends?

1 Is Chilly a big white bear?

2 Is Stuffy yellow?

3 Does Lambie like getting dirty?

4 Is Hallie a hippo?

Answers are on page 65.

Stuck Up

Beep, beep! Doc's brother Donny and his friend, Will, were using their toy trucks to build a big mountain of sand.

But when the sand collapsed and Will's digger, Riggo, got buried, there was a problem.

"Riggo's scoop is stuck!" said Will.

"Let Doc look at it," Donny told his friend. "She's real good at fixing things."

Donny called Doc and she came to help.

"Doc McStuffins at your service," she said.

"Please take real good care of Riggo," said Will.

Doc took Riggo and his friend Buddy into the play castle. Inside, her magic stethoscope made the toys come alive, so they could walk and talk.

"It's toy fixing time!" said Doc.

Buddy was worried. He and Riggo were a team, and they both needed to be able to work.

But Doc reassured him. "I'm as good at being a doctor for toys as you are at building things," she told him. "Let's do a check-up and try to figure out what's wrong."

Doc checked Riggo's ears and eyes, then she measured him, and listened to his heartbeat.

"Everything looks normal so far," she said. Then she took out her little hammer to test his reflexes.

"It won't hurt," said Doc, and she showed Riggo how it worked by tapping Lambie's leg.

If a little lamb like Lambie could be brave, so could a big digger like Riggo!

Doc tapped Riggo's arm, but it didn't move. Doc still wasn't sure what was wrong.

Just then, Doc heard Donny and Will outside.

"Toys, go stuffed!" said Doc, and they stopped moving.

Donny ran into the play castle so fast that sand flew into Doc's eye. Ouch! That hurt!

This was a job for a real doctor, Doctor Mom! She used water to wash the sand out of Doc's eye.

That gave Doc an idea! Now she knew just how to fix Riggo!

Doc looked at Riggo's scoop through her magnifying glass, which makes things look bigger, and easier to see.

"I have a diagnosis," she said, and drew a picture in her Big Book of Boo-Boos. "It's Sandyscoop Syndrome! Riggo has sand in his joints. That's what made his scoop get stuck!"

"Can you fix me?" asked Riggo.

"Ab-so-lute-ly!" said Doc.

Doc had a plan, but she needed help. "Here's what I want you to do," she told Buddy.

Buddy gave Stuffy, Lambie and Squeakers a ride to the drinking fountain, where they filled Squeakers with water. Then they squirted a big jet of water at Riggo's scoop to wash the sand away. Now he could move his scoop again.

"My scoop is working again!" Riggo said happily. "You're the greatest, Doc!"

Doc giggled. "I know," she said. "But I didn't do it all by myself."

Doc explained her diagnosis to Donny and Will when they arrived and said, "But it was nothing that Doc McStuffins couldn't fix."

Riggo and Buddy got back to work. But now they knew they had to be careful around sand.

"Good job, Doc," whispered Lambie. "Sometimes I really, really, really love my job!" smiled Doc.

Spot the Difference

These pictures look the same, but 10 things are different in picture 2. Look hard – can you spot all the differences?

1

2

Answers are on page 65.

Stuffy Gets a Check-up

Doc has special things to help her find out what's wrong with her patients. Can you draw lines from each thing Doc uses to the part of Stuffy she uses it on?

Doc listens to heartbeats using her **stethoscope.**

Doc uses an **otoscope** to look inside ears.

The **hammer** tests movement in knees.

The **wraparound arm cuff** measures blood pressure.

Answers are on page 65.

Helpful Hallie

Hallie just loves being helpful!
Colour in her picture. The little spots
show you which colours to use.

Lookin' Good!

Count with Doc

1 How many pairs of scissors can you see?

Count, and circle the number.

1 2 3 4 5

2 Are there 5, 6 or 7 crayons? Write a number.

3 Count the hearts and colour in the number.

1 2 3 4 5

4 How many notepads can you count? 2 or 3?

5 Draw more flowers to make 4.

Match the Pairs

Draw lines to join things that are the same.

What is left over?

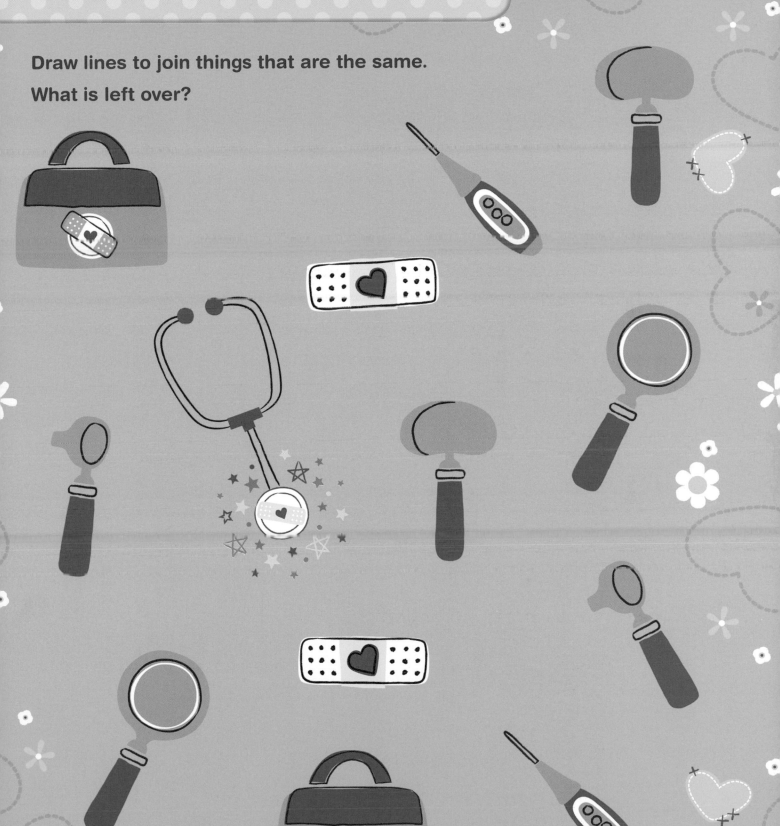

Answers are on page 65.

19

Doc's Friends

These pictures of Lambie look the same, but 1 is different. Can you find the odd one out?

a

b

c

d

e

f

Baa-baa brilliant!

20

Only 2 pictures of Stuffy
are exactly the same.
Can you find them?

Rrrrroar!

Answers are on page 65.

21

Out of the Box

One day, Doc showed Emmie Big Jack, her jack-in-the-box, and turned his key. "Watch!" said Doc.

Ting-a-ling-a-ling went the box, and – pop! – up popped a clown!

Doc showed Emmie a smaller box. "And this is Little Jack!"

Emmie just loved Little Jack! "Make him pop up!" she cried.

But this time, when Doc turned the key, the music was slow and sad.

The lid opened, and a little clown appeared, but he didn't pop up.

"That's weird," said Doc. "He usually pops up just like Big Jack."

When Emmie went home, Doc took Little Jack to her clinic.

"The Doc is in!" said Doc, and as her magic stethoscope glowed, the toys came to life.

"OK, guys," said Doc. "We have a new patient."

Big Jack popped out to say hello, but Little Jack only peeped out of his box. He had no pop!

"You OK, Little Jack?" asked Big Jack.

"I can't pop like I usually do," said Little Jack sadly.

"That's why you're here to see the Doc," said Big Jack. "She's gonna figure out what's wrong with you."

When Doc tried to examine Little Jack he pulled back into his box and slammed the lid shut!

"Maybe he's afraid to get a check-up," said Lambie.

"Are you?" asked Big Jack.

"I've never had one before," said Little Jack.

"It won't hurt," said Doc. "I'm here to help you feel better."

"And I'll be here if you need a cuddle," said Lambie.

In the check-up room, Doc said, "You wanna pick out a sticker for when you're done, Little Jack?"

Yes he did! "Stickers!" yelled Little Jack. "I LOVE stickers!"

Doc smiled. "OK," she said. "Let's find out what happened to your pop."

Doc opened Little Jack's box and shone her otoscope light inside. "Ooo, I see the problem!" she said. "Your clothes are stuck in your music box. That's why you can't pop up. I have a diagnosis! This is a case of **Cantpopitis!**"

Doc drew a picture in the Big Book of Boo-Boos.

"Now we have to get you unstuck!" said Doc, reaching into Little Jack's box and tugging at his clothes. "Almost got it ... there!"

With his clothes free, Little Jack popped all the way up – pop!

"I can pop again!" he cried happily. "Thanks, Doc!"

A little later, Doc went to Emmie's house.

"I have something to show you,"
said Doc, turning Little Jack's key.
   Up he popped with a big, **BIG** pop!
   Emmie was delighted. "You fixed it!"
she said. "Do it again! Do it again!"
   So Doc turned the key again ...
and again ...
      and again ...
         and – ting-a-ling-a-ling –
Little Jack popped out each time: pop!
pop! pop!
   "Good as new!" said Doc.

Chilly the Snowman

"Brrrrrrrr! Drawing is cool!"
says Chilly. Draw and colour in Chilly's
hat, eyes, nose, mouth and buttons.

Great colouring!

Write your name
on the line.

Chilly the Snowman

by_____

What Comes Next?

Hallie likes to keep Doc's clinic tidy. Today she's making patterns. Can you draw the next thing in each row?

1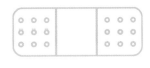

2

3

4  

5

Answers are on page 65.

Can You Solve the Clues?

When Doc has a patient, she looks for clues to find out what's wrong so she can fix it. Look and listen for clues to help you answer these questions.

1 Can you guess this patient's name?

a   **Rabbit Ray**

b   **Robot Ray**

c   **Rag doll Ray**

2 When someone comes along and Doc needs the toys to go back to being stuffed, what does she tell them to do?

3 Boppy couldn't stand up because air kept escaping through little holes in his skin. He had a bad case of – what?

a   Pricklethorns

b   Hiccups

c   Tummy ache

4 The doll at Doc's tea party had Eyeswideitis. Her name begins with s and ends with e. What is she called?

a   Maisie

b   Sara

c   Suzie

6 What sound does Lambie's friend Squeakers make?

a   roar

b   growl

c   squeak

5 What is Lenny the fire engine's number?

Answers are on page 65.

29

You Need a Kiss!

A kiss can make you feel better!
Colour in the picture, then add lots more kisses!
✗ ✗ ✗

Lambie

Looks like you need a cuddle!

Colouring in the Clinic

Join the dotted lines to draw
something Doc uses in her clinic,
then colour it in.

Doc uses this machine
to measure her patients.

Happy to Be Healthy!

Hey, everybody, it's Doc here!
Do you know how to stay healthy?
Let's find out!

1 To keep from spreading germs, what should you do?

2 What should you do if you get a splinter?

a   wash your hands

b   play Hippo bounce

c   have a tickle fest

a   knock down building blocks

b   tell an adult so they can
    take it out

c   throw balls at Stuffy's tummy

3 When you're out on a really hot day, what should you do?

a give Boppy a hug

b trumpet like an elephant

c drink plenty of water

4 When you get tired and lose your energy, what should you do?

a have a tea party

b take a nap and recharge

c play basketball

The DOC is in

5 What should you do to keep your breath fresh?

a play in the water

b ride a plastic horse

c brush your teeth

Answers are on page 66.

Hallie Hasn't Heard

 Doc
 Hallie
 Lambie
 Stuffy
 Chilly
 Squeakers

Listen to this story about Hallie's ears. When you see a picture, say the name out loud.

Oh, dear! was having trouble with her ears.

"Didn't you hear me calling?" asked .

"Did you hear call?" asked the toys.

 , and all nodded, yes. O-oh!

"I'm worried about ," said .

"Me, too," said . "And me," said .

 decided to find out what was wrong.

 put her stethoscope tips in 's ears.

"Close your eyes,"  told . "Raise

your hand when you hear squeak."

Squeak! heard a loud squeak.

 Squeak! But didn't hear a quiet squeak.

 used her otoscope to look in 's ears.

Now knew what was wrong! "You have

Earstuffinosis," said . "There's

some extra stuffing in your ears, .

They're a bit blocked up, so the

sound can't get through."

 gently pulled out some stuffing, and that

did the trick: now could hear again!

To celebrate, , , , and

 played Hide and Go Seek. Who was IT?

Can you guess? Yes, ! "I'm gonna use

my eyes AND my ears to find you!" said .

" 1 2 3 4 5 6 7 8 9 10. Here I come!"

I Spy ...

Sometimes Doc has to take a VERY close look at her patients! That's when her magnifying glass comes in handy because it makes things look MUCH bigger than they really are!

1

a   b   c   d

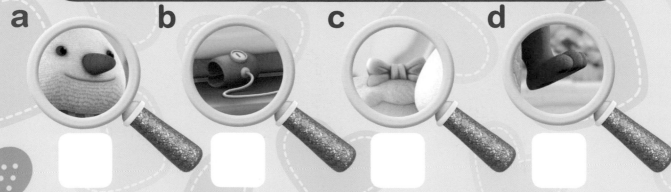

Take a close look at the little pictures at the bottom of these pages.

Which ones can you find in pictures 1 and 2?

Tick ✔ ONLY the ones you can see.

a

b

c

d

Answers are on page 66.

39

Hide and Go Seek

The toys love playing Hide and Go Seek.
You can play with them! Close your eyes, and count:
1 2 3 4 5 6 7 8 9 10
Say, "Ready or not, here I come!"
Can you find their hiding places?

Chilly

Stuffy

Hallie

40

When you find the toys, point, tick ✔ a box, and say:

Found you, Chilly!

Found you, Stuffy!

Found you, Hallie!

Found you, Lambie!

There's something else hidden — Doc's bag. Where is it?

You're good at this game! Now it's your turn to hide. Can you find a good hiding place?

Answers are on page 66.

Lambie

41

Count with Stuffy

Oh, no, Stuffy dropped all Doc's plasters!
"I meant to do that!" said Stuffy –
but he didn't really, did he?
Help him sort out the plasters.
Count ones that are the same colour,
and write numbers in the answer boxes.

Pink is Doc's favourite colour. Which colour do you like best?

Answers are on page 66.

42

Let's Be Friends

Finish colouring in the picture of Hallie, Lambie and Stuffy as neatly as you can.

Friendship is the #1 best medicine

Rescue Ronda, Ready for Takeoff!

Poor Chilly! When Donny threw him up into the air he got stuck in the basketball hoop! He needed someone to rescue him.

It was lucky that Donny's friend Luca arrived with his helicopter, Rescue Ronda. She can fly, and her job is rescuing toys. Toys like Chilly!

Donny and Luca worked Ronda's controls. But Donny made her go left, and Luca made her go right, and Ronda went out of control, and crashed into a bush!

Now her propellers wouldn't spin.

"And the rescue basket fell off!" said Luca, reaching into the bush to get it. But, "Ow!" he said, pulling his hand back. "That hurts!"

When Donny took Luca to let Mom fix his hand, Doc put on her stethoscope and the toys came to life.

Doc stood on a stool to rescue Chilly, then she took Rescue Ronda to the clinic.

"First I'm going to listen to your engine," she told her patient.

Whirr! Ronda's engine was fine.

Whirr-whirr! So was her tail propeller.

The problem was Ronda's main propellers.

"They just won't spin!" said Doc.

She tapped the propellers, then looked under them.

"Did anything weird happen to you today, Ronda?" Doc asked.

"Well, I did crash into that bush ..." said Ronda.

Then Doc went to see how Luca was getting on. He had a splinter in his finger, but Mom soon got it out.

"Be careful next time you reach into a bush," Mom told Luca.

Now Doc knew what had happened!

She ran back to the clinic. "You got a splinter from the same bush as Luca," Doc told Ronda. "I have a diagnosis," she said. "Ronda, you have stuckpropatosis."

"StuckpropaWHATsis?" asked Ronda.

Doc explained. "You have a little tiny twig, like a splinter, stuck in your propellers. You got it when you flew into the bush."

That sounded serious! "Can you fix it, Doc?" asked Ronda.

"I sure can!" said Doc, holding up her tweezers. "OK, I'm going to get the splinter out."

Ronda was scared, so the toys tried to make her feel brave.

"Doc is the best splinter-puller I know," Lambie told her.

That did the trick! "OK, Doc," said Ronda.

Doc soon got the splinter out. "Does that feel better?" she asked Ronda.

"Af-firm-a-tive!" said Ronda. "Let's give these rotors a spin!"

Rmm, rrrrmm! Ronda's engine revved, then her propellers started to spin, and she lifted off the ground. "We have liftoff!"

Stuffy was so excited that he got tangled up in Ronda's rescue ropes.

"Leave this rescue to me," said Ronda, and she flew Stuffy to safety. "Great rescue, Ronda!" said Doc as Donny and Luca arrived.

"Toys, go stuffed!" said Doc.

Ronda zoomed around. "You fixed her!" said Luca. "Thanks, Doc."

"Just doing my job," said Doc. "Rescue Ronda, ready for takeoff!"

47

Shadows!

Draw lines to match the shadows to the toys.

48

The Search is On!

Oh, no! Doc has lost some of her medical instruments! Can you help Stuffy, Chilly and Lambie find them for her? Follow the lines with your finger, then draw over them.

Answers are on page 66.

Jigsaw Pictures

Which piece is missing from the jigsaw picture?
Write the letter in the white box.

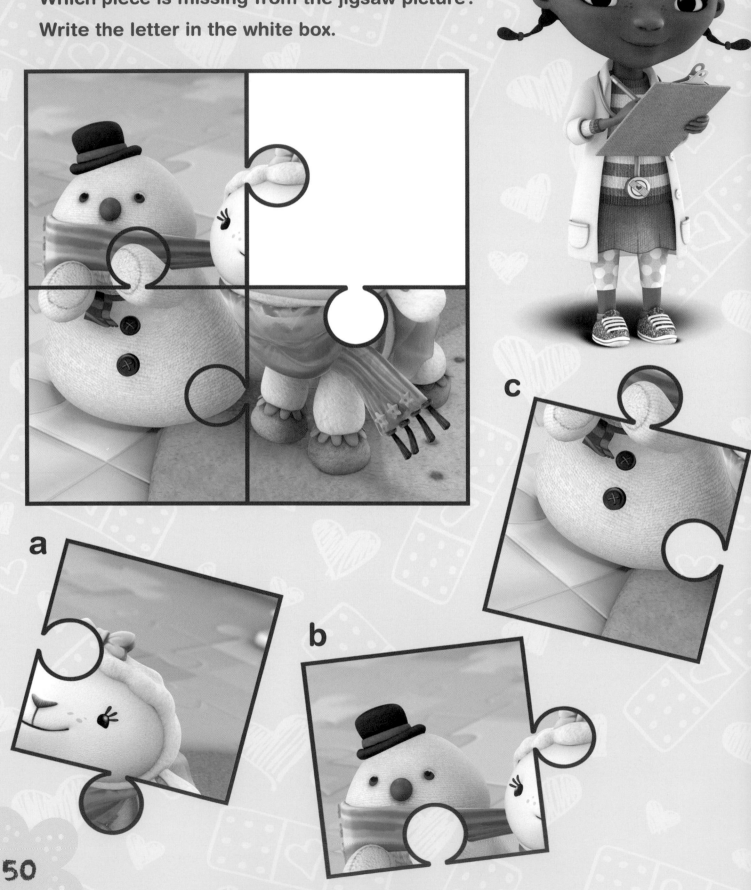

a

b

c

50

Which 2 jigsaw pieces are missing this time?

Write the letters in the white boxes.

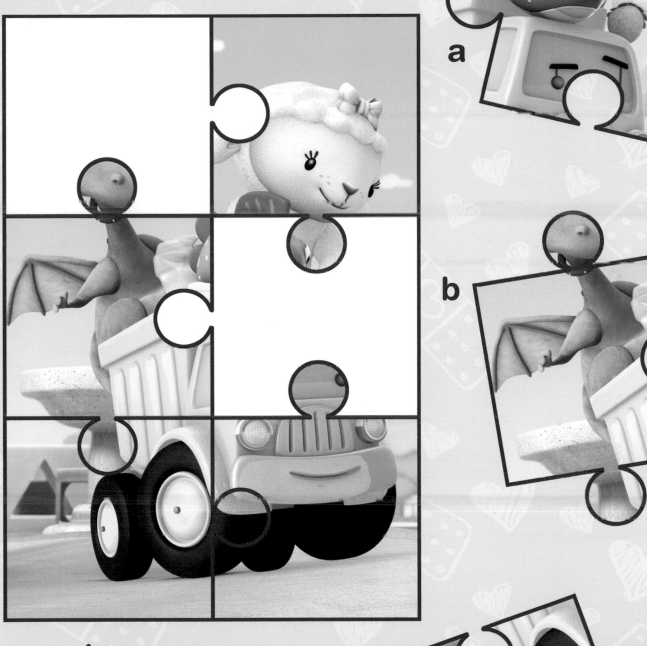

Answers are on page 66.

Toys, Go Stuffed!

Only Doc – and you! – know that she can make toys come to life. It's a secret, so when someone comes along, Doc says, "Toys, go stuffed!"

Play with a friend. Say, "Go stuffed!" and keep as still and as quiet as you can. Don't blink, move, or giggle, because the first one to move or make a sound is OUT and the other player is the winner.

HAVE CUDDLES. WILL SHARE.

Copy Colour

"Need a cuddle, Stuffy?" Lambie asks her friend.
Use the little picture to help you colour in the big one.

Who Am I?

Doc looks for clues to find out what is wrong with her patients.
Which sets of clues are about Globo, Chilly, Squeakers and Bronty?

1 I can swim.
I have yellow spots.
I squeak!
Who am I?

2 I am green.
I have 6 arms.
I have blue ears.
Who am I?

Chilly

Squeakers

Bronty

Globo

3 I am white.
I have no bones.
I have an orange nose.
Who am I?

4 I am blue.
I am very big.
I am a dinosaur.
Who am I?

Answers are on page 66.

Chilly

STAY COOL

Doc

BOO BOOS gone!

© Disney

The Big Book of Boo-Boos

When Doc finds out what's wrong with a patient, she says, **"I have a diagnosis!"** and draws a picture and writes a name in the Big Book of Boo-Boos.
Can you match the Boo-Boo pictures to their names? Write a letter in each box.

1 Driedout-a-tosis

2 Pricklethorns

3 Dustie Musties

Doc likes teamwork! Be part of her team by drawing a Boo-Boo picture.

Answers are on page 66.

Walkie-Talkie Time

One day, Donny and Henry were playing with their walkie-talkies. They were pretending to be sneaky spies, spying on Doc!

Scre-e-e-e-ch! But Donny's walkie-talkie made weird noises.

"This thing doesn't work!" he whispered. "Henry, can you hear me?"

"No!" replied Henry. "My walkie-talkie's making a weird noise."

"Now we'll never be able to sneak up on Doc," said Donny.

"Yes, we will!" said Henry. "I've got spy goggles. We'll use them!"

They went to get them, leaving the walkie-talkies behind.

Doc and the toys were in the clinic when Donny's walkie-talkie jumped up at the window.

"**Aaagh!**" said Chilly. "Th-th-there's something out there!"

Doc looked. "I don't see anything."

"I must be seeing things!" said Chilly. "I'd like a check-up, please, Doc."

The walkie-talkie jumped up again, and this time Doc saw it, and opened the door.

In jumped Walter the walkie-talkie. "Is Gracie here?" he asked, worried. "She's my other half. When I talk, she listens. When she talks, I listen. I can't find her. When I press my talk button all I hear is this screechy noise!"

"That noise is called static," said Doc. "It's why you can't talk to Gracie. You need a check-up."

Doc used her pen light to check Walter's batteries.

She listened with her stethoscope and pressed his buttons.

Then she looked through her magnifying glass and saw – a hole!

She held up a mirror to show Walter. "My antenna's gone!" he cried.

"Diagnosis, **staticosis!**" said Doc, drawing a picture in her Big Book of Boo-Boos. "Walkie-talkies need antennae to hear each other from far away. Without his antenna, Walter hears static instead of Gracie's voice."

Doc and the toys searched for the antenna. Walter found it, and Doc fitted it back on.

"Gracie, are you there?" said Walter.

"Walter, is that you?" came a sad voice. "I'm all tangled up in some plants. And there are lots of red berries, too!"

"Red berries?" said Doc. "I know where she is!"

Doc went to the strawberry patch. "Gracie's in here," she said.

They soon found Gracie and Walter explained what had happened.

"Doc fixed my antenna so we can hear each other again."

Just then, Doc heard Donny and Henry. "Quick, everyone, go stuffed!" she said.

"GOTCHA!" Donny and Henry jumped out wearing spy goggles.

Doc played along. "You got me, all right!" she said, handing the walkie-talkies to Donny and Henry.

"The ... walkie-talkies ... are ... fixed," said Doc. "I ... repeat. The ... walkie-talkies ... are ... fixed!"

"Cool! Thanks!" said Henry.

"Walkie-talkies and spy goggles. Now we can spy on anyone!" said Donny. "Look. I see Dad! Let's sneak up on him."

Doc smiled a big smile. Job done!

Race to the Clinic!

Who will be first to get to the playhouse clinic?
Play with a friend. Roll a dice and
move from space to space.

Tip: use buttons or coins as counters.

If you land on ...

go back 2 spaces

have an extra throw

go on 2 spaces

go back to the start

start

finish

I Totally Knew That!

Stuffy wants to do this quiz, but he needs your help, because he doesn't know all the answers!

1 Who is Doc's brother? Is his name Danny or Donny?

No, Really! I DID!

2 In the story Stuck Up on page 10, whose scoop got stuck? Was it Riggo or Buddy?

3 In the story Rescue Ronda on page 44, is Ronda a fire engine or a helicopter?

4 What job does Doc's Mom do?

5 How many fish can you see in the waiting room tank?

6 How many buttons does Chilly have?

7 In the story Out of the Box on page 22, is Little Jack a rabbit or a jack-in-the-box?

8 Which of Doc's friends wears red glasses?

Answers are on page 66.

Answers

pages 8-9
Say Hi To Doc and Her Friends

1. False, Doc is a doctor for stuffed animals and toys
2. True
3. True
1. No, a snowman
2. No, Stuffy is blue
3. No, Lambie hates getting dirty
4. Yes, she's a hippo

pages 14-15
Spot the Difference

page 16
Stuffy Gets a Check-up

page 18
Count with Doc

1. 4; 2. 6; 3. 5; 4. 3; 5. 2 + 2 = 4.

page 19
Match the Pairs

pages 20-21
Doc's Friends

Lambie d. Stuffy b, d.

page 27
What Comes Next?

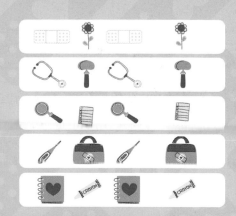

page 28
Can You Solve the Clues?

1. b
2. "Toys, go stuffed!"
3. a
4. c
5. 9
6. c

Great answers! Baa-baa brilliant!

Answers

pages 34-35
Happy to Be Healthy!
1. a; 2. b; 3. c; 4. b; 5. c.

pages 38-39
I Spy ...
1. a, c, d; 2. a, b, c.

pages 40-41
Hide and Go Seek

page 42
Count With Stuffy
4 blue; 2 yellow; 5 green; 3 pink.

page 48
Shadows!

page 49
The Search Is On!

pages 50-51
Jigsaw Pictures
1. a; 2. a, d.

page 54
Who Am I?
1. Squeakers; 2. Globo;
3. Chilly; 4. Bronty

page 57
The Big Book of Boo-Boos
1. c; 2. a; 3. b.

page 64
I Totally Knew That!
1. Donny
2. Riggo's scoop got stuck
3. Helicopter
4. She's a doctor
5. 3
6. 2
7. Jack-in-the-box
8. Hallie

I have a diagnosis! You have good-at-puzzles-itis!

T. L. C.

TENDER Loving CARE

Prescribing hugs cuddles and kisses